Pete the Cat 5-Minute Bedtime Stories

by Kimberly & James Dean

HARPER

An Imprint of HarperCollinsPublishers

Pete the Cat 5-Minute Bedtime Stories

Text copyright © 2020 by Kimberly & James Dean

Illustrations copyright © 2020 by James Dean

www.harpercollinschildrens.com

Library of Congress Control Number: 2019950276

ISBN 978-0-06-329774-6

Book design by Lori S. Malkin

22 23 SCP 10 9 8 7

❖

First Edition

Contents

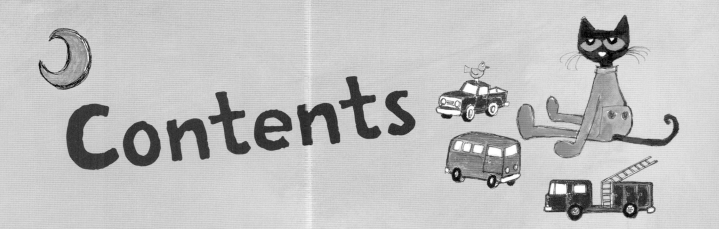

Pete the Cat and the Bedtime Blues

Pete and the gang are at the beach. They've been having a groovy time in the surf and sand. But now the sun is starting to set.

Pete is bummed out. He doesn't want the fun to end. But what can he do? They can't surf in the dark!

Then Pete has an idea. "Hey," he shouts. "Why should our fun end just because the sun is tired? Let's have a sleepover at my house. That will give us more time for tons of fun!"
Pete's friends love that idea.
"Groovy!" says Gus.

"Will there be snacks?" asks Alligator.
Grumpy Toad points to his motorcycle. "Come on, let's go to Pete's place!"

The party at Pete's house is far-out! The gang
orders pizza and plays and plays and plays.
Alligator throws around Pete's soccer ball.
Gus goes for a ride on Pete's bike.
Grumpy Toad drives Pete's remote-control car.
And Pete draws with his crayons.

Finally, the friends decide it is time for bed.

The gang rolls out their sleeping bags and puts on their pajamas.

"Good night, Gus," Pete says, turning off the light. "Good night, Alligator. Good night, Grumpy Toad."

"Good night, Pete," the friends call.

Pete pulls his blanket up high. He fixes his sleeping cap. He squishes around to get comfortable. It has been a long, groovy day, but now he is ready for some shut-eye.

Slowly, Pete's eyes close. He is about to catch
some ZZZs when he hears a noise.
Clap! Clap! Clap!
Pete sits up and turns
on the lights. "Who did
that?" he asks.

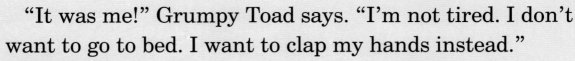

"It was me!" Grumpy Toad says. "I'm not tired. I don't want to go to bed. I want to clap my hands instead."

Pete covers his head. "Let's clap tomorrow," he says. "Right now, this cool cat needs to go to bed."

Pete turns off the light again. "Good night, Gus. Good night, Alligator. Good night, Grumpy Toad. Time to sleep!"

"Good night, Pete!" the friends call.

Pete fluffs up his pillow. He pulls his blanket down. Then he closes his eyes.

Pete is about to catch some ZZZs when he hears another noise.

Rat-a-tat-tat.

Pete turns on the lights again. "Who did that?" he asks.

11

"It was me!" says Gus. "I'm not tired. I don't want to go to bed. I want to jam."

Pete shakes his head. "That *was* a cool beat, but let's rock out tomorrow instead," he says. "This cat needs his sleep!"

Pete turns off the light again. "Good night, Gus. Good night, Alligator. Good night, Grumpy Toad. Time to sleep!"

"Good night, Pete!" the friends call.

Pete rolls onto his left side. He rolls onto his right side. He is about to catch some ZZZs when he hears a loud *munch*.

Pete knows that sound. He is sure it is Alligator. He is always up for eating.

Pete turns on the light. Sure enough, Alligator is munching on a piece of pizza.

Pete sighs. What can he do? All the clapping, rat-a-tat-tatting, and munching are giving him the bedtime blues!

Then Pete has an idea. He gets out his favorite bedtime story and begins to read.

As he reads, Pete notices that the room is quiet. There is no more clapping, no more rat-a-tat-tatting, and no more munching.

Pete looks up. His friends have gathered around him. They want to hear the story, too.

Pete turns back to the beginning of the book and begins to read it aloud.
His friends settle down and listen. No one makes a sound.

Pete yawns as he turns the last page of the book.
He has been so focused on the story, he didn't even
notice his friends creep off to their own beds.
"Good night. Sleep tight," he whispers.

Pete puts his book down. He turns off the lights. And he closes his eyes.

Soon, Pete is fast asleep. Dreams of another groovy day of surfing fill his head as the cool cat finally catches some ZZZs.

Pete the Cat and the Lost Tooth

Oh no! Pete lost a tooth. What should he do?

Pete shows the tooth to his mom.

"Put the tooth under your pillow," she says. "The Tooth Fairy will come and give you money for it."

Pete thinks under his pillow is a
strange place for a tooth. But his mom
is usually right. And it would be pretty
cool to meet the Tooth Fairy.

Pete puts the tooth under his pillow.
Then he closes his eyes and
pretends to sleep.

Suddenly, he hears a jingling
noise. Pete opens his eyes.
The Tooth Fairy is at his
window!

The Tooth Fairy flies into Pete's room. She looks worried.
"What's wrong?" Pete asks.

"It's a very busy night," the Tooth Fairy explains. "I don't know how I'm going to collect all the teeth that fell out today."

Pete jumps up. "I can help!" he says.

The Tooth Fairy thinks that is an awesome idea. With a flick of her wand, she gives Pete magic wings. Now he can fly, just like her.

Pete loves his new wings. He zips around his room and does loop-the-loops in the air. "Groovy!" he shouts.

Finally, Pete settles down. "So," he says, "what do I have to do?"

The Tooth Fairy gives Pete a list of names. "You need to visit each of these cool kids to get their teeth."

1. Callie
2. Alligator
3. Gus

The Tooth Fairy gives Pete two bags. One is full of teeth, and one is full of coins.

"Take the tooth and put it in this bag," she says. "Then leave a coin from *this* bag under the pillow."

Pete looks at the bag of teeth. It already looks full. "How will I fit any more teeth in here?" he asks.

The Tooth Fairy smiles. "Oh, I wouldn't worry about that. Being a tooth fairy comes with a certain kind of magic!"

"Far out!" Pete says. He is ready to go!

Pete's first stop is Callie's house. He flies through the window and straight to her bed.

Pete lifts up Callie's pillow. He takes her tooth and leaves behind a coin.

Next up is Alligator's house.

Pete finds Alligator's tooth. It is big and sharp! He pulls it out from under the pillow and puts a coin in its place. Then Pete sneaks back out the window.

Pete smiles to himself. This job is easy.

Pete's last stop is Gus. He flies inside and reaches under Gus's pillow. Uh-oh. There is no tooth!

Pete looks next to Gus's drums. He looks in Gus's drawer. He even checks inside Gus's baseball mitt. The tooth is nowhere to be found!

Does Pete panic?
Nope!
He just keeps looking for the tooth!

Just then, Gus wakes up.

"Gus!" Pete cries. "I have been looking everywhere for your lost tooth. Where is it?"

"My tooth?" Gus asks.

Pete nods. "I'm supposed to get it for the Tooth Fairy!"

"But, Pete," Gus says, "platypuses do not have teeth."

Gus opens his mouth and shows Pete. "See?"

"Far-out," Pete says. "No teeth at all!"

Gus shrugs. "Sorry. It would have been nice to join in the Tooth Fairy fun."

Pete smiles. "No worries," he says. He takes a coin from his bag and slips it under Gus's pillow.

"Thank you," says Gus.

"You're welcome," Pete says. "Good night!"

Pete leaves Gus's room and heads home. On his way, he comes across the Tooth Fairy.

"All done?" she asks. "Did you have any trouble?"

Pete shakes his head and holds out the two bags. "Nope. Everything went great. That was awesome!"

"Thanks, Pete," the Tooth Fairy says. She takes the bags. "I should be getting to my next house."

As Pete makes his way home, he thinks about Gus.
Not everyone is the same. But being kind is always cool.
That sounds like the perfect title for his next song. . .
.

Pete the Cat
Out of this World

Pete is very happy. He has been chosen for a super-groovy mission. He is going into outer space! He will be the first cat to walk on the moon.

But first, Pete has to train. . . .

Pete goes in the zero-gravity chamber. He spins and spins and spins.

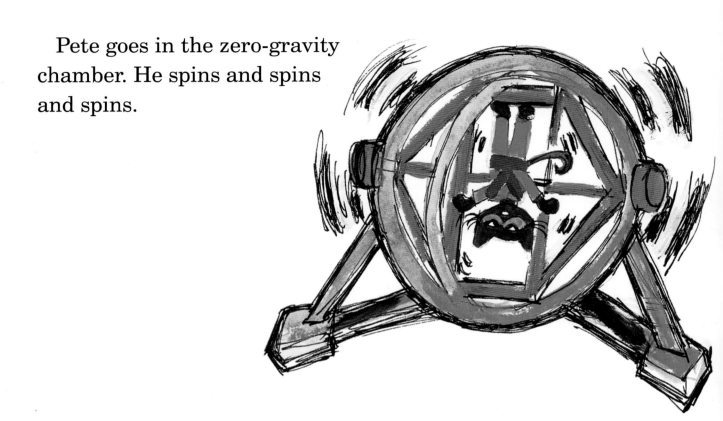

He learns how to drive a rover. Pete practices picking up small rocks.

Pete goes to Mission Control. He learns how the astronauts speak to the crew on Earth. He learns how the rocket gets into space. And he learns how it lands.

Finally, Pete is ready.

Pete and the other astronauts climb into the space capsule. They buckle in and prepare for the flight.

Five . . .

Four . . .

Three . . .

Two . . .

One . . .

Liftoff!

The ship shakes and rattles. A loud sound fills the cabin.

Pete looks out the window. They are speeding through outer space! Super cool!

The ship blasts past a satellite. A comet streaks by the window.

The Earth grows smaller as the astronauts make their way to the moon.

The trip to the moon takes a long time.

Pete brings out his guitar. He plays a groovy interstellar song for the other astronauts.

The astronauts float through the cabin to the beat of Pete's song.

Mission Control listens in.
"Cool beat, Pete!" they say.

Finally, the rocket lands on the moon.

Pete straps on his space suit. He opens the door and climbs down the ladder. His feet touch the ground!

Pete and the other astronauts walk around. It's time to explore.

Pete looks at the surface of the moon. It's
bumpy and kind of dusty—nothing like the
ground at home. He climbs into the rover. He
uses his training to drive over the surface of
the moon.

Pete collects moon rocks to bring back to
Earth and maps the moon's surface.

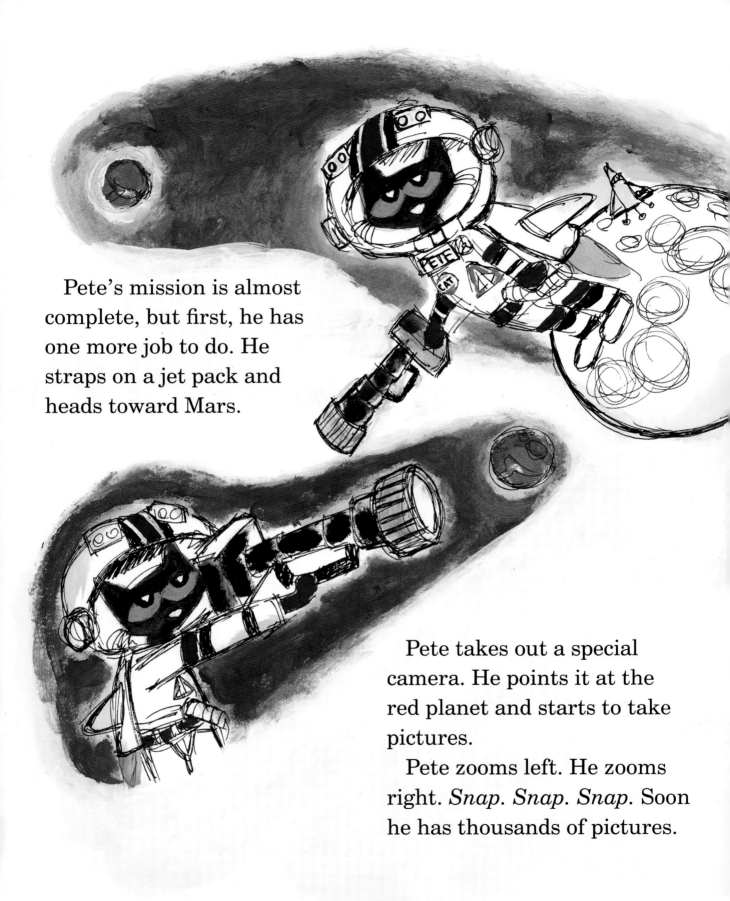

Pete's mission is almost complete, but first, he has one more job to do. He straps on a jet pack and heads toward Mars.

Pete takes out a special camera. He points it at the red planet and starts to take pictures.

Pete zooms left. He zooms right. *Snap. Snap. Snap.* Soon he has thousands of pictures.

Oh no! Pete lost track of time. He has drifted too far away from the moon. He has to make it back before the ship takes off for Earth!

Pete refires his jet pack. He zooms toward the moon's surface. If he does not make it back, he will be stuck in space forever!

Phew! Pete makes it back just in time! The other astronauts are already in the ship.

Pete climbs aboard and straps himself in.

The ship shakes and rattles as it takes off.

Pete looks out the window. The moon grows smaller as the astronauts begin their journey back to Earth.

Finally, the ship reaches the Earth's atmosphere. It touches down and taxis to a stop.

Mission Control cheers. They are glad to have their astronauts home safe, and they can't wait to see the pictures and rocks Pete collected.

Pete's trip to outer space was out of this world. He's psyched to have his feet back on solid ground, but he hopes he gets to go up again soon. Mars seems like a groovy place to explore next. . . .

Rocket on, Pete!

Pete the Cat Goes Camping

Pete is going camping with his family. This is his first camping trip. He can't wait! Camping sounds groovy!

Pete and his brother, Bob, pack the car. They bring food, flashlights, fishing poles, and tents.

"Don't forget the sleeping bags!" says Dad. He hands them to Pete.

It is a long drive to
the campsite. Finally,
they arrive.

Pete's mom and dad
set up the tents.

Pete and Bob go
deep into the woods.
They collect sticks
to make a campfire.

Pete and Bob decide to go for a hike. Bob shows Pete the footprints of all the animals who live in the forest.

They see bear tracks and deer tracks. One set of tracks looks like it belongs to a raccoon. Just then, a bunny hops past. He leaves another set of tracks in the dirt.

Pete looks at a big footprint. "Far-out," he says. "Look how big this is, Bob!"

Bob bends down. "I don't know *what* animal made that," he says. "But I bet it's not something we want to run into!"

Bob and Pete make their way back to the campsite. Their dad is waiting for them.

"Come on, boys," he says. "It's time to catch our dinner!" Pete's dad holds up a fishing rod. "Who wants to try?"

Bob doesn't like fishing. He stays at the campsite to get the fire going.

Pete wants to try. He and his dad go to the lake. They have to be very quiet so they don't scare away the fish.

Finally, Pete feels something tug on his line. He caught something!

Pete and his dad bring their catch back to the campsite.
"That was awesome," Pete says. "Look what I caught!"
Pete's mom takes the fish from him. She cleans it and
cooks it over the campfire. It is delicious. Great job, Pete!

After dinner, Pete and his family gather around the fire to keep warm. It is getting dark out.

Pete looks up at the sky. He has never seen so many stars before!

"How about a story?" Pete's dad asks.

Bob jumps up. "I've got one!" he shouts. Bob tells Pete and his parents all about a big, hairy giant who lives in the woods. "Every night, he prowls the campsites, looking for snacks," Bob says. "In the morning, all that's left are crumbs . . . and giant footprints. In fact, his feet are so big that he is called Bigfoot!"

"Groovy story, Bob," Pete's mom says. "And speaking of snacks, who wants a s'more?"

Pete's dad gives everyone a stick to toast marshmallows on. Pete's mom hands out graham crackers and chocolate.

Soon everyone is enjoying a yummy dessert.

Pete can't stop thinking about Bob's story. What if Bigfoot is real?

"Don't let Bob scare you," Pete's mom says. "No one has ever seen Bigfoot."

"But if he is real," Pete's dad adds, giving Pete another marshmallow, "I bet he's friendly. And I bet he likes s'mores!"

That gives Pete an idea. He decides to make a s'more for Bigfoot. That way, if he *does* come, he'll have a tasty snack.

Soon it is time for bed.
Pete's dad puts out the fire,
and Pete and Bob head
to their tent.

Pete snuggles into his sleeping bag. It's warm and cozy, but he can't sleep. The woods seem extra dark, and all the forest sounds seem extra loud!

Suddenly, Pete hears a weird swooshing sound. He sits up and looks around.

"Bob," Pete says. "What is that?"

Bob opens one eye and listens closely. "It's just the wind," he says finally.

Pete still can't sleep. He hears a strange hooting sound.

"It's just an owl," Bob says.

That makes Pete think of his friend Owl. He starts to feel better, but then he hears a loud chirping sound.

"It's just the crickets," Bob says. "Go to bed, Pete!"

Pete puts his pillow over his head. Maybe he can hide from the noises.

Crack!
Pete sits up again. "Bob, did you hear that?" he asks.
But Bob is fast asleep.

Pete hears another *crack*! He listens carefully. Is it Bigfoot?
Pete opens the tent and looks around, but it is too dark to see
anything.

The next morning, Pete is the first one up. He rushes
outside and looks around. He doesn't see any broken
branches. There aren't any footprints. . . . Then Pete sees
the table. The s'more he left for Bigfoot is gone! In its place
is a note. It says *Thanks for the treat!*
XOXO and is stamped with the biggest
footprint Pete has ever seen!

Pete shows the note to his family.

"I knew Bigfoot was real!" Bob shouts.

Pete smiles. He knows now that Bigfoot isn't scary.
Just because he looks different doesn't mean Pete should
be afraid of him.

Pete starts looking for sticks. He can't wait to make
another s'more for his groovy new friend, Bigfoot.

Pete the Cat and the Treasure Map

Pete and Callie are having a sleepover. "Hey, Dad," Pete says. "How about a groovy bedtime story?"

Pete's dad smiles. "You bet," he says.

"It all began on a ship . . . a pirate ship! Captain Pete and First Mate Callie were on the trail of the treasure of Secret Island. . . .

"Captain Pete steered the ship through the big waves, the wind pushing at the sails.

"'Let's go, mateys,' said Captain Pete. 'We'll be there in no time!'

"Suddenly, First Mate Callie spotted something in the water. It was a big green head! 'What's that?' she asked.

"Just then, the boat began to rock. A giant arm reached up and splashed at the water, making waves that crashed down onto Captain Pete's boat.

"'Arrrrgh!' yelled the crew. 'It's a monster! Run for your lives!'

"But did Pete worry? Not at all! He knew just what to do.

"Captain Pete raced belowdecks. When he came back, he was holding his guitar. 'That monster isn't trying to hurt us,' he said. 'He's rocking a cool beat!'

"Captain Pete began to rock out on his guitar. The monster nodded its head along with the music. Then it began to splash its arms in time to the music.

"'See,' said Captain Pete. 'He's not a scary sea monster at all. He's an awesome sea drummer!'

"'Oh no,' First Mate Callie shouted as it started to rain. 'Look. Lightning! There must be a storm coming.'

"'Batten down the hatches,' Captain Pete shouted. 'Everyone get ready. This looks like it's going to be a big one!'

"The boat began to rock back and forth. The wind picked up, and the waves grew taller and taller. Soon, Captain Pete's boat was on top of the waves.

"'Whoa,' said Captain Pete as a wave almost knocked over the boat. 'This is *not* a groovy storm!'

"Just then, Captain Pete had an idea. 'Hey there, friend,' he yelled to the sea monster. 'We need some help!'

"The monster grabbed the ship and held it up, high above the water. The wind continued to lash the boat, but the crew was safe. The waves couldn't topple them as long as they were in the monster's grip.

"Slowly, the wind died down and the water went back to normal.

"'Hip, hip, hooray! Hip, hip, hooray!' shouted the crew as the monster set them back in the water. 'Let's hear it for our new pal!'

"'Thanks, friend,' said Captain Pete. 'We never would have made it through that storm without you.'

"The monster grinned. He was happy to have helped his new buddies.

"Suddenly, First Mate Callie spotted something in the distance. It was Secret Island. 'Land, ho!' she shouted.

"The pirates rushed to look over the side of the boat. All that wind had moved them to exactly where they wanted to be!

"On the beach, Captain Pete found his friend Grumpy Toad. He was surrounded by a glittering pile of treasure!

"'Ahoy, mateys,' called Grumpy Toad. 'I see you found my treasure map. I wanted to keep all of this treasure for myself, but it's no fun if there's no one to share it with. Come join me. There's plenty to go around.'

"The crew jumped off the boat and ran to land. 'Thanks, Grumpy Toad,' they shouted.

"But Captain Pete wasn't happy. He was glad to have found the treasure, but something was missing. This was a celebration, and that meant music!

"The pirates loaded all the treasure onto their ship. Then Captain Pete got out his guitar again.

"'Hey,' Captain Pete shouted. 'Where's our drummer?'

"The sea monster popped his head out of the water and began splashing a beat.

"'Rock on!' said Captain Pete, matching the monster's pace. 'What a cool song!'

"The crew agreed. Soon they were all dancing to the music.

"Captain Pete and his crew set sail for home,"
Dad finished. "Their adventure was over, and so
is your bedtime story. Time for bed!"

Pete smiled to himself as he drifted off to
sleep. "A pirate's life for me. What an adventure
that would be!"

Pete the Cat
and the Tip-Top
Tree House

Pete the Cat has been busy. He has been building a tree house. Now it is finally done. But a tree house isn't any fun without friends to play with.

Pete calls his friends. "Come over," he tells them. "I built a groovy tree house for us to share!"

"Cool!" Callie says when she sees the tree house. "Let's play!"

Callie climbs the ladder and goes inside.

"Swingin'," says Marty as he jumps down from a branch and into the house.

Grumpy Toad and Emma join their friends inside.

Last but not least, Pete climbs the ladder. But when he gets to the top, there's nowhere to go! The tree house is too small. He can't fit inside!

"No worries," says Pete. "It's okay. I can fix it!"
Pete gets out his hammer. He finds some more
wood. Soon he is busy making the tree house bigger.
"This balcony is just what we need," he tells his
friends. "We'll be ready to play in no time."

Callie sticks her head out the door and calls to Pete, "Do you want some help?"

"Sure!" Pete says.

Callie carries some more wood up to Pete.

Marty swings onto the roof. "Neat balcony," he says. "But how about a tower?"

Pete loves that idea. Together, he and his friends add a tall tower to the tree house.

"This is such a great tree house!" Marty says. "Let's have a party, so we can really enjoy it."

"A party?" asks Pete. "But . . . what will everyone do?"

Emma climbs onto the balcony. "I can help with that!" she says.

Emma shows Pete a blueprint for the tree house.
While Pete was building the tower with Callie and
Marty, Emma was busy figuring out what else they
could add.

"Look at that," says Pete. "You really thought of
everything. This looks like the most far-out tree
house ever!"

Pete and his friends have a lot of work to do. They gather up their tools and get started.

Marty saws more wood.

Pete drills while Callie hammers.

Even Grumpy Toad helps. He carries wood up and down and tightens all the screws he sees.

Meanwhile, Emma keeps an eye on the plans. She makes sure everything is built according to her drawing.

The first room the friends finish is an arcade. They fill it with all their favorite games.

"Ooh, watch this!" Marty shouts as he plays *Big Banana*. "I'm going to get the high score!"

But Pete is not ready to play. "Come on," he says, "we still need to build the rest of the rooms!"

Pete and his friends get back to work.
They build a bowling alley with twenty lanes!
They build a wave pool for surfing indoors.

They build a movie theater and a skate park and a rock climbing wall and an ice rink.

"Wow," Pete says when they're done. "There are so many fun things to do, I don't know where to start!"

Callie wants to go bowling first.
Pete brings her over. He gets her a ball and sets up the pins.

Emma wants to go to the movies.
Pete helps her find a seat and brings her popcorn.

Grumpy Toad wants to try out the skate park.

Pete helps him find a skateboard that is just the right size.

Marty wants to go surfing.

Pete brings him to the wave pool and gets him a surfboard.

Pete is tired from running back and forth. He has been so busy helping his friends, he hasn't had a chance to try any of the cool rooms himself. Even worse, he's all by himself.

Pete calls his friends. "This is supposed to be a party," he says. "But we're all alone. Everyone come down."

Everyone climbs down.

"This tree house is amazing," says Callie, "but it's lonely playing by myself."

"I'm glad we built it," says Pete. "But for now, maybe we can stick to the jungle gym, right here on the ground."

Pete's friends agree.
Building the tree house was fun,
but being together is even more fun!

Pete the Cat and the Cool Caterpillar

Pete is on a bug hunt! He searches his backyard for something cool. Finally, he spots something. There is a caterpillar on the flowerpot.

"Groovy," Pete says. He scoops up the caterpillar and brings it inside to show to his parents.

"You'll need a safe place to keep that little guy," Pete's mom says. She helps him find a big glass jar.

Dad pokes lots of tiny holes in the lid. "He'll need air to breathe," Pete's dad explains. "And he'll need something to eat!"

Pete goes into the yard. He comes back with leaves for the caterpillar to eat and a twig for it to crawl on. He puts them in the jar. Then he carefully puts in the caterpillar.

"There you go, little guy," Pete says. "I hope you like your new home."

Pete puts the lid on the jar and brings it to his room. He wants the caterpillar to be the last thing he sees at night and the first thing he sees in the morning.

That night, Pete has dinner with his parents. He brushes his teeth and puts on his pajamas. Then he climbs into bed.

"Good night, Mom," says Pete. "Good night, Dad. Good night, caterpillar. Sleep tight. I'll see you in the morning!"

But when Pete wakes up in the morning, the caterpillar is not in its jar.

"Mom! Dad!" Pete calls. "It's gone! My caterpillar is gone!"

Pete's parents come to look at the jar.

"I don't understand," Pete says sadly. "The lid is still on. Where could it have gone?"

Pete's dad looks inside the jar. Then he starts to smile. "Your caterpillar isn't *gone*, Pete," he says. "It's just changed."

Pete's dad points to a sack hanging from the twig. "That's called a pupa," he says. "The caterpillar is in there."

Pete looks at the jar. "Will it stay in there forever?" he asks.

Pete's mom shakes her head. "No, it won't. It's changing into something else. Just give it time. You'll see."

"What is it going to become?" Pete asks.

"It's a surprise," Pete's mom says. "Be patient. It will be worth the wait."

That afternoon, Callie
comes for a visit.

"What's in the jar?" she
asks Pete.

"It *was* a caterpillar," Pete says. "Mom said it will turn into
something else . . . eventually."

Callie looks at the jar. "When do you think it will change?"

Pete shrugs. "Soon, I hope."

The next day, Gus comes over.

"Did it change yet?" he asks.

Pete shakes his head. "Not yet."

A few days later, Marty visits.

"Anything yet?" he asks.

Pete shakes his head again. "Nothing. It just hangs there, not
doing anything at all!"

Pete waits . . . and waits . . . and waits. The caterpillar seems to be taking *forever* to change.

"Mom," Pete says. "How can you be sure it will do something?"

"It will," says Pete's mom. "Just be patient."

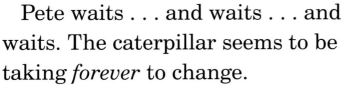

"Dad," Pete says. "What if there's something wrong with the caterpillar? What if it *can't* change?"

"It can," says Pete's dad. "It just takes time. You'll see."

Pete studies the jar. He hopes his parents are right.

Then, suddenly, the pupa begins to shake.

"Mom! Dad!" Pete shouts. "It's happening!"

As Pete watches, the pupa cracks and something starts to move around.

A head pokes out, then some legs, and two colorful wings.

The caterpillar has changed into a beautiful butterfly!

Pete and his parents bring the jar to the park. It's time to set the butterfly free.

Pete opens the jar and the butterfly flutters into the air. It flaps around in a small circle and comes to a rest right on Pete's nose.

Pete giggles. "That tickles," he says.

The butterfly sits there for another moment, and then flaps its wings and flies away.

Pete looks up at it. He is sad to see his new friend go, but he is also happy for the butterfly.

"Goodbye, butterfly," he calls. "I'll miss you."

The next day, Pete heads back out to the park. He sees all of his friends. Now *they* are on a bug hunt!

"Your caterpillar was so cool, I want to see what I can find!" Callie says. "So far I found this big pile of ants. Look, they're building an anthill."

"Groovy," Pete says.

"I found a ladybug," says Gus. "Look, it has nine spots."

"Nice!" Pete says.

"Hey, Pete," Marty calls. "Take a look at this spider. It caught a fly!"

"Neat!" says Pete.

"Want to watch it with me for a while?" Marty asks.

Pete shakes his head. "No thanks," he says.

"I'm off to find another caterpillar!"

Pete the Cat Checks Out the Library

Pete's mom is taking him to the
library for the first time.

"Hi!" Pete greets the librarian. "I'm looking for the perfect
bedtime story!"

The librarian smiles. "I think I can help you with that," she says.
"But first, you're going to need a library card!"

"Cool!" Pete says. "My own card?"

"That's right," says the librarian. "Just for you. Now, how about
we find you that book?"

113

The librarian takes Pete to her favorite room. There
are lots of Pete-sized chairs and tables and shelves.
There is fun art on the walls. And there are more books
than Pete has ever seen in one place!

"What do I do now?" he asks.

"Now you try to find something you like," the librarian says. "You can bring home any book in here. When you're ready, just bring the books you like to me, and I'll help you check them out."

Pete goes over to a shelf and chooses a book about jets. He reads it and pretends he's a stunt pilot. He flies a superfast jet and does a loop-the-loop high in the sky.

"Wheee!" Pete shouts.

Next Pete picks a book with a wizard and a unicorn on the cover.

Pete pretends to be a wizard. He helps the brave knights fight off an evil dragon and goes for a ride on a unicorn.

Pete practices his wizard spells. "Take that!" he cries, shooting a blast of magic at the dragon.

Pete's next book is about bugs. He pretends to be a scientist, studying spiders and ants.

Pete looks through his microscope at the microscopic world around him. He's never seen anything so cool before. He wonders what great discoveries he'd make as a scientist.

Pete picks up a book of monster stories. He imagines himself facing off against the big, bad wolf.

Pete does not like that story. He quickly puts the book down. Reading that at bedtime would give him bad dreams!

Pete's next book is about Egypt. He reads all about the pyramids and imagines himself discovering a long-lost pharaoh. Pete rides his camel across the desert and climbs to the top of the tallest pyramid. He even takes a ride aboard the Sphinx.

Pete thinks being an explorer would be a great adventure.

Pete picks a book with a robot on the cover. He imagines that *he* is a robot.

"Bleep. Bloop. Bleep," Pete says.

He moves his arms and legs like a robot. They make a funny whizzing sound as he glides across the room.

Pete begins to dance. It is a robot dance party!

Next Pete reads about superheroes. He imagines
flying around the city in a cape, chasing bad guys,
and saving the day.

All of Pete's friends cheer for him.

"Thank you," Pete says, "but it's all in a day's
work."

Super Pete to the rescue!

Pete chooses a book about the ocean. He imagines himself on a submarine, learning about marine life. He sees whales and octopuses and dolphins.

"Watch out for that fish!" Pete calls as a fish swims by.

The world under the ocean is amazing! Pete is glad to have learned more about it.

"So," says the librarian, interrupting Pete's fantasy. "Did you pick one?"

Pete shakes his head. "No," he says. "I picked them all!"

Pete's mom smiles. Tonight is going to be one long bedtime!

Pete the Cat's Train Trip

Pete loves trains. He loves the way they look. He loves the way they sound. He even loves the way they smell.

Now Pete is going to visit his grandma . . . and he gets to *ride* on a train!

129

Pete's mom buys three tickets. She gives one to Pete, one to Bob, and keeps one for herself.

"Keep these tickets safe," Mom says. "You won't be able to ride the train without them."

Pete holds his ticket tight. He can't believe it. His very first train ticket! He hopes he gets to keep it.

Inside, Pete waits impatiently for the train.

"Is it time yet?" he asks.

Mom shakes her head. "Not yet," she says.

"How about now?" Pete asks.

Pete's mom brings him to the train board. It shows where all the trains are going and what time they arrive at.

"Our train comes at ten o'clock," she says.

Just then, a train pulls into the station.
"Is that it?" Pete asks.

Bob shakes his head. "Sorry, Pete. That one's going in the other direction."

Another train speeds through the station without stopping.

"What happened?" Pete asks. "Why didn't it stop?"

"It's a cargo train," Bob explains. "It carries *things* from place to place, not passengers."

Finally, Pete's train arrives. The doors
slide open, and the conductor steps out.

"All aboard!" he shouts.

Pete follows his mom onto the train. As they walk, he looks
around. The train is full of passengers. It's so exciting.

Pete's mom finds three seats. "Here we are, boys," she says.

"I can't wait to see Grandma," Bob says.

"I can't wait to explore the train!" says Pete.

133

"A fan of trains, are you?" the conductor says, collecting Pete's ticket. "I always liked them, too. Ever since I was a boy, I've been a big fan."

"I love trains!" Pete says. "This is my first time on one."

The conductor hands Pete's ticket back to him. "Well, then you'll want to keep this so you'll always remember your first time on a train."

The conductor moves on to collect the rest of the passengers' tickets. But he isn't gone long. A few minutes later, he comes back with a gift for Pete. It's an engineer's hat!

The conductor places the hat on Pete's head. "How about a tour of the train?" he says.

Pete grins. "Far-out!"

Pete follows the conductor from car to car. The ground rumbles under his feet.

"This," says the conductor when they reach the last car, "is the caboose."

Pete looks out the window. They are going over a bridge. "Groovy!" he says.

Next the conductor leads Pete to
the front of the train.
"Come in!" says the engineer.
Pete walks in and
looks around. "Wow!"
he says.

The engineer shows Pete the engine. He shows Pete the
train's brakes.

Pete looks out the front of the train. Everything looks so
different from up here. "Look!" he says. "A tunnel!"

Pete watches through the window as they go through the tunnel. The train's light shines on the track.

"Hey, kid," the engineer says. "Want to give the horn a try?"

Pete can't believe it. "You bet!" he says.

Toot! Toot!

"That was awesome!" Pete says.

As Pete makes his way back to his seat, he meets the other passengers on the train. They are all going different places for different reasons.

Pete plays a game with one of the passengers.

He sings a song with another. What a groovy ride!

Finally, Pete gets back to his seat.

"There you are," Pete's mom says. "Our stop is next."

Pete climbs onto his seat and looks out the window.

Slowly, the train station comes into sight.

On the platform, Pete sees his grandma. As soon as the train comes to a stop, he races out to greet her.

"Grandma, Grandma," Pete shouts. "I got to see the caboose, and the engine, and honk the horn!"

Pete's grandma gives him a big hug. "That sounds like quite the exciting trip!" she says.

Pete hugs his grandma back. "It was," he says, "but I'm glad we're here now. I love trains, but I love being with you even more."

Pete the Cat and the Surprise Teacher

Pete wakes up and stretches. It's time to get ready for school.

Pete eats his breakfast. He puts on his red shoes and his backpack. And he grabs his lunch.

"Ready to go?" Pete's dad asks.

Pete looks around. He doesn't understand why his dad is taking him to the bus. "Where's Mom?"

Pete's dad smiles. "She has a surprise for you."

Pete climbs on board the bus and finds a seat next to Callie.

"Hi, Pete. What's new?" Callie asks.

"My dad brought me to the bus this morning," Pete says. "He says my mom has a surprise for me. I wonder what it is."

The bus pulls up to the school, and Pete and Callie get out. As soon as they get to their classroom, Pete sees the surprise. His mom is standing at the front of the room!

"Hi, class," she says. "I'm Mrs. Cat.
I'm the substitute teacher today."
Pete grins. "Groovy!"

Pete's mom takes attendance. She reads the morning's announcements. Finally, it is time for lessons to begin.

"I'm going to need all of your help today," Pete's mom tells the class. "What is your first lesson?"

"First, we go to art!" says Pete.

Pete's mom smiles. "Thank you, Pete," she says.

"Okay, class," says Pete's mom. "Everyone line up in single file at the door. Now follow me. Art, here we come!"

The class follows Pete's mom out the door. They head down the hallway and stop at the first room they see.

Pete's mom opens the door and leads the class inside.

Uh-oh. This isn't the art studio. It's the gym!

There is already another class in the gym, but the coach doesn't mind. "Come on in and play with us," he says. "There's always room for more!"

Pete's mom isn't sure. They are supposed to be in art class. "Pleeeease," the class begs. Finally, Pete's mom agrees.

Pete and his friends change into their gym clothes. Then they join the other class. They are playing basketball.

"Wow!" Pete says. "Gym class is way cooler with more kids!"

Pete's mom looks at the clock. It's time for the
next lesson.

Pete and his friends change back out of their gym
clothes, and she leads them to the next classroom.

Uh-oh. This isn't art. It's music!

There is already another class in the room, but the
music teacher doesn't mind.

"Stay and sing," she says. "We can always use more
voices."

Pete gets out his guitar and starts to strum an awesome beat. The other kids sing along.

"Far-out," Pete says. "Listen to how much louder we are with more kids!"

The music teacher smiles. "You kids are welcome to come sing with us anytime. Way to rock out, Pete!"

Just then, Pete's stomach starts to grumble.
He's hungry.

Pete's mom looks at the clock. It's time for lunch!

Pete's mom brings the kids back to the classroom to get their lunches. Then they head to the lunchroom. But Pete's mom takes a wrong turn, and they end up on the playground!

"Oh no," she says. "This isn't right at all."
Pete and his friends think it's great.
"Let's have a picnic!" Pete says.

When they are done eating, Pete and his friends clean up the picnic.

"Now it *must* be time for art," Pete's mom says. "Pete, I keep going to the wrong room! Can you lead the way this time?"

Pete leads the class to the art room. When they get there, they find another class already hard at work.

"I'm sorry we're late," Pete's mom tells the art teacher. "I got a little confused. Is there enough room for us to join you?"

The art teacher shakes his head. "Sorry," he says. "We're all out of space. Besides, the day is almost over."

"Bummer," Pete says. "Now what do we do?"

Pete's mom leads the kids back to the classroom. "I'm sorry you missed art today," she says.

Just then, Pete has an idea. "We didn't make it to the art studio, but we can still do art here," he says. "Look! We've got everything we need. Crayons, paper, scissors . . ."

Pete's mom thinks that's a great idea. "Okay," she says. "We'll make our own art!"

Pete gathers his friends together. He has a plan.

The kids start drawing cat faces. Pete colors them in, and Callie cuts them out.

On the other side of the room, Pete's friends write something on a big piece of paper.

Finally, their project is done.

"Surprise!" the class shouts. They made a banner for Pete's mom.

Pete's mom is touched. No one has ever done anything so nice for her.

"We may have done things all wrong today," Pete says, "but we had the grooviest day ever. Thanks for being our teacher."

Pete hugs his mom. "And thanks for being my mom," he whispers.

Pete the Cat: Firefighter Pete

Pete has a secret. He has been training after school to be a firefighter. Now his whole class is going on a field trip to the firehouse. Pete climbs onto the bus with his friends. He can't wait to show off his new skills!

The bus parks next to the bright red firehouse.

"Wow!" Callie says. "Look how big it is!"

Callie's right. The firehouse is huge! It's so big it can hold two long red fire trucks and all of the firefighters' equipment.

"Can we go inside?" Pete's friends shout.

Pete's teacher smiles. "Of course," she says. "That's why we're here!"

"Hiya, Pete," a firefighter says when the kids go inside. "Hi, kids."

Callie turns to Pete. "How does he know your name?" she asks.

The firefighter points to Pete. "Why, Pete here is one of our top trainees. Come on, Pete, let's show your class what it means to be a firefighter. First, you'll need your gear."

As Pete puts on his boots, the firefighter tells the kids what each thing is for.

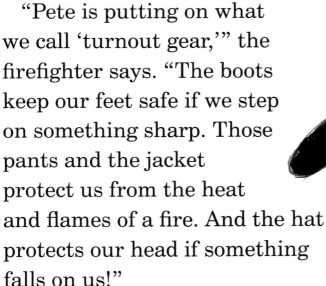

"Pete is putting on what we call 'turnout gear,'" the firefighter says. "The boots keep our feet safe if we step on something sharp. Those pants and the jacket protect us from the heat and flames of a fire. And the hat protects our head if something falls on us!"

Pete shows off his full gear. It's so heavy, he can barely move!

Pete takes off his gear, and he and the firefighter show his class the rest of the station.

The firefighter gives each kid a chance to ring the old brass bell outside the firehouse.

Then the kids take turns sliding down the firefighters' pole.

"Wheee!" Callie cries as she glides down. "This is fun!"

The firefighter even lets the kids sit in the fire truck. Callie sits in the driver's seat. She presses the horn. *Brrrrrt!* The sound is so loud, everyone covers their ears.

Then she turns on the sirens and lights. *Wooo-eeee! Wooo-eeee!* The lights flash red and yellow.

"Wow, Pete," Callie says. "I can't believe you get to do this all the time. It's awesome!"

Just then, a loud bell rings in the firehouse.
It's the fire alarm. There's a fire in town!

The firefighters scramble into their boots and
helmets and say goodbye to the kids.

"Come on, trainee Pete," they shout. "We've
got a fire to put out!"

Pete quickly puts his own gear back on, too.

Pete and firefighters hop into the truck. They turn
on the lights and sirens and race out of the firehouse.
The fire is all the way on the other side of town.
They need to get there . . . fast!

Wooo-eeee! Wooo-eeee!
The fire truck's sirens wail as the truck races through town. The other cars hear it coming and move out of the way.

The fire truck goes through red lights and green lights. There's no time to waste!

Pete looks out the window. He's been training for weeks, but this is his first real fire. He can't wait!

Finally, the crew reaches the site of the fire. It's an old building.

Pete looks up. The flames are huge! He's never felt anything so hot before.

Pete hops out of the truck. He knows what he has to do.

Working with the other firefighters, he hooks up the fire hose to the fire hydrant. Now the firefighters have water to fight the fire.

The firefighters attach another hose to the fire truck.
Pete gives the signal, and the firefighters turn on the water.

Whoosh! The water gushes out of the hose.

Pete and other firefighters hold the hose tight. With so
much water coming out, it's hard to control it!

Slowly, the fire starts to go out. But now there is smoke everywhere. It's hard to see!

Suddenly, Pete hears a shout on the roof. It's Grumpy Toad. He's stuck on top of the building!

The firefighters raise a long ladder from the truck. They rest it against the side of the building and begin to climb.

Pete and another firefighter help Grumpy Toad climb down the ladder carefully.

Pete brings Grumpy Toad over to a waiting ambulance. It showed up while the firefighters were putting out the fire. The medics are waiting for Grumpy Toad. They check him out to make sure he is okay. Meanwhile, the firefighters put out the last of the fire.

Back at the firehouse, the firefighters take off their gear.

"Great job, Pete," they say. "You fought your first fire! What did you think?"

Pete grins. "That was far-out," he says. "When can we do it again?"

Pete the Cat's Groovy Bake Sale

Pete's school is having a bake sale! Pete is excited. He wants to bring something to sell.

Pete thinks about what *he* likes to eat. He likes cookies. He likes brownies. He likes pie and marshmallow treats and ice-cream sundaes. Pete likes *all* sweets. But which one should he make for the bake sale?

Finally, Pete makes a decision. He'll make cookies!

Pete gets out the ingredients: eggs, flour, sugar, butter, and, of course, chocolate chips!

He gets out a big bowl and a mixing spoon.

Pete is ready to get to work!

Pete cracks the eggs and drops them in the bowl. He melts the butter and adds it, too.

Pete puts in the flour, the sugar, and the chocolate chips. He mixes it all together.

Uh-oh! The cookie dough goes everywhere! Pete made a big mess.

Does Pete worry? Not at all! He cleans up the mess and rolls the dough into balls, which he places on a cookie sheet.

Pete's mom turns on the oven. When it's warm enough, she helps him put the cookies in.

Pete watches through the oven door as the cookies slowly get bigger. A yummy smell starts to drift through the air.

Just then, Bob bounces into the house. Pete starts to talk to him and forgets all about his cookies!

Suddenly, Pete starts to smell something not-so-yummy. It's the cookies. Some of them are burning.

Pete's mom helps him take the cookies out of the oven. Some of them are okay, but most of them are too burned to eat.

But does Pete worry? Not at all. He comes up with another plan for a treat to sell at the bake sale.

Pete tries to make ice-cream sundaes. He gets out a big glass. He gets out the ice cream and the whipped cream and the chocolate syrup.

Pete carefully scoops the ingredients into the glass. But making the perfect creation takes too long. His ice-cream sundae turns into ice-cream soup!

Pete tries to make a pudding pie, but he doesn't have enough crust.

Pete checks the cabinet. He used the last of his flour making the cookies. That means he can't make cake or muffins, either.

Pete looks around. The kitchen is a big mess, but he still has no treats for the bake sale.

"What am I going to do now?" Pete asks his mom. "I promised Callie I'd bring something for the bake sale."

"You'll find something yummy to make," Pete's mom says. "You always find a way."

Pete looks at what he has left. He sees some berries, some vanilla pudding, some milk, some whipped cream, and a few pieces of cookie.

Pete has an idea.

"Everything here is yummy," he says. "I'll just use a little bit of all of it. If I do that, I'm sure I'll end up with a yummy treat."

Pete cleans up the mess he made. He gets rid of all the treats that didn't work. Finally, all he has left are the ingredients for his new treat.

Pete pours the pudding mix and milk into a bowl and
stirs. After a few minutes, the pudding starts to take shape.
Next, he adds the whipped cream and the strawberries.
Finally, Pete puts in the unburned pieces of cookie.
Pete looks at his creation. It looks yummy to him!

Pete goes back to the cabinet and pulls out a muffin tin. He slowly scoops his new creation into the tin, being careful not to make another mess.

Pete smiles as he finishes the last scoop. He is proud of himself. He took what he had and made a tray of tasty, groovy berry goodness.

Pete opens the refrigerator and puts the tray inside. He'll leave it there overnight to chill.

The next day is the bake sale. Before Pete goes to school, his mom helps him scoop the treat into pretty cups. The two load the cups into a tray, and Pete's mom walks him to the bus stop.

"Good luck at the bake sale," Pete's mom says, kissing him on the head.

At school, Pete unloads his treats onto his table at the bake sale. Then he waits for someone to come over.

All around him people are selling cookies and brownies and cupcakes. No one has anything like Pete's treat!

"Wow, Pete," Callie says, coming over to his table. "What's that?"

Pete hands Callie a cup and a spoon. "I call it Groovy Berry Goodness," he says.

Callie takes a bite. Pete's treat is delicious! She rushes to tell the other kids all about it.

Soon, all of Pete's treats are sold . . . all but one.

Pete keeps the one cup of his Groovy Berry Goodness. When school is over, he brings it home.

"I saved this for you," he tells his mom. "Thanks for all your help. And for being the grooviest mom around!"